Copyright © 2006 by NordSüd Verlag AG, Gossau Zürich, Switzerland
First published in Switzerland under the title *Wer hilft dir, Osterhase?*
English translation copyright © 2006 by North-South Books Inc., New York

First published in the United States, Great Britain, Canada, Australia, and New Zealand
in 2006 by North-South Books Inc., an imprint of NordSüd Verlag AG, Gossau Zürich, Switzerland.
Distributed in the United States by North-South Books Inc., New York.

Library of Congress Cataloging-in-Publication Data is available.
A CIP catalogue record for this book is available from The British Library.

ISBN-13: 978-0-7358-2054-8 / ISBN-10: 0-7358-2054-6 (trade edition)
10 9 8 7 6 5 4 3 2 1

Printed in China

Hide,
Easter Bunny,
Hide!

By Udo Weigelt
Illustrated by Cristina Kadmon
Translated by J. Alison James

NORTHSOUTH
BOOKS

New York / London

Easter Bunny was nearly finished decorating his eggs
when Squirrel and Woodpecker burst into his workshop.

"Quick, Easter Bunny," cried Squirrel excitedly. "You have
to hide! A *masked bandit* is after you! He's asked all
the animals where to find you!"

"How very strange," said Easter Bunny. "What could
he possibly want with me?"

"I don't know," said Woodpecker, "but you better hide!"

"I can't hide *myself*," Easter Bunny said in despair. "Easter is tomorrow! I have eggs to hide!"

"Then we'll hide the eggs for you," Squirrel offered. "You can stay safely at home."

Before he had a chance to think about it, Squirrel and Woodpecker were on their way, taking Easter Bunny's eggs with them.

"Hide myself," grumbled Easter Bunny. "I don't want to hide myself. I like hiding eggs for Easter." Before he could think anymore about it, a deep voice called out from the bushes. "Easter Bunny!" Terrified, Easter Bunny grabbed a paintbrush to defend himself.

"At last I found you!" said the voice, as he emerged from the bushes. Masked, yes, but this was no bandit. It was just Raccoon, with his masked eyes.

Easter Bunny was very relieved. "I did wonder who could be chasing me," he said with a chuckle. "My friends said a masked bandit was after me."

"Masked bandit indeed," said Raccoon.

"Well, well," said Easter Bunny, "I guess you really *shouldn't* believe everything you hear. But why were you looking for me?"

"Here's my problem," explained Raccoon. "Last year, my children saw you hiding eggs. Now they want their own Easter egg hunt, but we have no eggs. Could you help us?"

"Of course I'll help you," Easter Bunny said. "But my eggs are all gone. They've already been hidden."

"But I thought you were in charge of hiding the eggs yourself."

"Of course I am, usually. But this year, my friends are doing it for me."

How odd, thought Raccoon. "Are you sure you're the *real* Easter Bunny?" he asked.

"Don't be silly, of course I'm the real Easter Bunny! You know what," Easter Bunny suddenly decided, "we'll just go get some of the eggs for your little ones. There are plenty." Together, they ran off.

When they reached the little park by the town, they found Squirrel and Woodpecker.

"We're already finished," said Squirrel, proudly.

"And who is this?" asked Woodpecker, looking nervously at Raccoon.

"This is the dangerous masked bandit you warned me about," said Easter Bunny. He explained everything to his friends.

"So where have you hidden the eggs," asked Easter Bunny. "We need three of them for the little raccoons."

"We thought we'd make it fun for the children," explained Squirrel. "So we hid the eggs high in the trees."

"What?" cried Easter Bunny. "In the trees? But people can't fly like birds or climb like squirrels. We'll have to hide all the eggs again—this time on the ground."

Oops! Squirrel and Woodpecker looked a little embarrassed.
They hadn't thought of that. Carefully, they brought all the eggs back
down from the trees.

"Is Easter always like this?" asked Raccoon, astonished.

"Usually not," said Easter Bunny. "But now we're running late.
I'll never have enough time to hide the eggs all by myself. Could
you please help, too?"

Everyone helped Easter Bunny hide the eggs in the grass and in the bushes. They finished just in time. Children were already coming to look for the eggs. Only three eggs were left.

"These are for your little ones," said Easter Bunny to Raccoon. "Thank you for your help!"

"I'm sorry I thought you weren't the real Easter Bunny," said Raccoon.

"I am the one and only," said the Easter Bunny. "And those two," he pointed to Woodpecker and Squirrel, "are official Easter Bunny Assistants. Just like you."

"Good-bye Easter Bunny . . . and Easter Bunny Assistants!" called Raccoon as he ran off to hide the eggs for his children.

"I hope you're not mad at us," said Woodpecker on the way home. "We were only trying to help."

"Of course I'm not mad at you," said Easter Bunny. "I have a secret—I hid an egg especially for each of you."

When they got back to Easter Bunny's workshop, Squirrel and Woodpecker started their Easter egg hunt. It took them a long time to find them. You see, the last place they thought to look was high up in the trees!